ARCHIE the BEAR
BECOMES A BIG BROTHER

WRITTEN BY
ROM NELSON

ILLUSTRATIONS BY
SVETLANA LESHUKOVA

Archie the Bear - Becomes a Big Brother
Published by The Life Graduate
www.thelifegraduate.com
Copyright © 2022 Rom Nelson
ISBN: 978-1-922664-49-5 (Paperback)
978-1-922664-48-8 (Hardback)
978-1-922664-50-1 (Ebook)

AN ORIGINAL BOOK BY

Thank you to my brilliant illustrator Svetlana for the exquisite illustrations throughout this book. You have brought Archie the Bear to life for millions of children across the globe.

To:

Congratulations!!

You are a Big Brother

....

....

....

....

....

Love From ....

Mommy and Daddy had a big surprise for me.

A brand new little baby, so cute and cuddly.

We all love to snuggle and keep cosy and warm.

We've become a family of four since baby was born.

Some time ago, I was a little baby bear too.

Helping Mommy and Daddy is something I love to do.

When I play with baby, I am always quiet with my toys.

Little babies don't like the sound of sirens and loud noise.

When baby gets changed, I hold onto my nose.

I quietly sneak out on my tippy toes!

Big splash, little splash, it's time for some fun.

The bath water splashes all over my mom!

When baby is tired, and it's time
for sleep,
I read my favourite book about
counting some sheep.

When I have a cuddle, I sing songs and nursery rhymes.

Snuggle time with baby is one of my favourite times.

When baby starts crying, I use my hands to cover my ears.
Mommy gently rocks baby to stop all the tears.

The crying can be quick or sometimes it's long.
Mommy soothes baby with her favourite song.

When visiting the park Daddy pushes me high.

Mommy and baby watch me reach for the sky!

I love baby bear because we can play together.

My new best friend and I'm now a big brother forever.

So goodbye from Archie and little
Baby Bear.

Sometime soon we'll have a new story
to share.

About the Author

Rom Nelson is a Best Selling Author and Founder of The Life Graduate Publishing Group. He commenced his career working in some of the most well-known schools in Australia, including Head of Faculty positions in Oxford and Wimbledon, United Kingdom.

Rom authored his first book back in 2009 and has now created several books and resources, including five that have become Best Sellers in the US, UK, Canada and Australia.

The 'Archie the Bear' Series has been created for toddlers in a fun and enjoyable hand-drawn picture storybook format, helping them to prepare for new experiences.

Using fun and creative rhyming language, Archie the Bear will help parents by taking their children through the experience so they are prepared and relaxed.

https://www.thelifegraduate.com/contact

ARCHIE the BEAR
ADVENTURES

ARCHIE the BEAR
THE BEACH ADVENTURE

ROM NELSON AND
SVETLANA LESHUKOVA

JOIN ARCHIE AND BABY BEAR FOR A VISIT TO THE BEACH FOR FUN IN THE SUN!

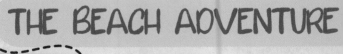

THE BEACH ADVENTURE

ARCHIE the BEAR

ADVENTURES

JOIN ARCHIE AS HE SHOWS TODDLERS HOW TO USE THE POTTY!

POTTY TRAINING

Printed in Great Britain
by Amazon

28705016R00018